ORCHARD BOOKS

First published in the USA by Scholastic Inc in 2017
First published in the UK in 2018 by The Watts Publishing Group

1 3 5 7 9 10 8 6 4 2

A CIP catalogue record for this book is available from the British Library.

ISBN 978 1 40835 482 7

Printed and bound by CPI Group (UK) Ltd, Croydon, CR0 4YY

MIX
Paper from
responsible sources
FSC® C104740

The paper and board used in this book are
made from wood from responsible sources.

Orchard Books
An imprint of Hachette Children's Group
Part of The Watts Publishing Group Limited
Carmelite House, 50 Victoria Embankment, London EC4Y 0DZ

An Hachette UK Company

www.hachette.co.uk
www.hachettechildrens.co.uk

THE POKÉMON SCHOOL

Adapted by Jeanette Lane

ORCHARD

CHAPTER 1

ALOLA ADVENTURE

"Yippee! Whoo!" Ash yelled. "AWESOME!"

Ash grinned as he gazed out at the wide, blue ocean. He felt a splash of water on his face. Melemele Island, one of several islands in the Alola region, was the perfect place for a holiday! He had Pikachu, his best friend and beloved Pokémon, on his shoulder. The island sun was warm and bright. What could be better?

The answer: zipping over the waves while riding a super cool Sharpedo! Sharpedo was the famous Alola Pokémon jet ski. Instead of a machine with a motor, it was a fabulous Water- and Dark-type Pokémon with super speed.

"Full throttle, Sharpedo!" Ash directed. With several strong flips of its powerful tail,

Sharpedo zoomed ahead.

This thrilling Sharpedo ride was just one of the amazing activities Ash could enjoy on Melemele Island. The Alola region was a tropical paradise, and it had all kinds of unique Pokémon. Even though Ash and his mum were on holiday, he was still thinking about Pokémon.

Ash loved nothing more than encountering new Pokémon. It was his goal to become a Pokémon Master. He had travelled to many regions on his quest to compete at top Pokémon Gyms, but he already knew that his time in Alola would be special.

While Ash and his mum were on Melemele Island, they had an important task. Professor Oak, the famous Pokémon Professor who lived in Ash's hometown in the Kanto region, had asked them for a favour. Professor Oak needed them to deliver a Pokémon Egg to his cousin, Samson Oak. It was a mysterious Egg, and Ash knew it was a very important job.

To get to Samson Oak, Ash and his mum took a taxi. But it wasn't just any taxi.

"My first Pokémon taxi!" Ash declared from the comfortable seat of a cart pulled by a strong Tauros. "This is the best EVER!"

Ash was thrilled. Pikachu made a happy squeak, and the Tauros replied with a friendly grunt. Also along for the trip was Mr. Mime, Ash's mum's Pokémon companion. Mr. Mime, a Psychic- and Fairy-type Pokémon, had actually won the tickets for their big island getaway!

"Here in the Alola region, we use the power of Pokémon to go anywhere and everywhere," the taxi driver explained. "We refer to these Pokémon as Ride Pokémon. When you travel on land, you take a Land Ride Pokémon. When you want to fly, you take an Air Ride Pokémon. On water, a Water Ride Pokémon."

Ash found it all fascinating. He loved learning new Pokémon facts!

His mum was more interested in the exotic fruit at the local market. She wanted to buy some berries, so the taxi driver pulled Tauros to a stop.

As Ash got out of the cart, he noticed something out of the corner of his eye. It wasn't fruit.

"It's a Pokémon," Ash murmured, rushing over to investigate. The Pokémon was halfway underground, with its tan-and-orange striped head poking out. "So cool!

I wonder what its name is?"

Ash leaned down, and the Pokémon reached out and pinched his nose with its strong pincer-like jaws.

As soon as the Bug-type Pokémon let go, it dove underground and dug an escape tunnel. "OK, let's catch it, Pikachu!" Ash cried, holding his sore nose.

In an instant, the two friends had rushed off into a nearby forest, leaving the market – and Ash's mum – far behind. They raced after the speedy Pokémon.

However, once they were deep in the forest, the Pokémon had too many places to hide. Tall, leafy trees rose high overhead, and lush plants grew all over the forest floor.

"Guess we missed it," Ash said, panting to catch his breath. Ash looked up and realised that he didn't know where he was. He thought about his mum. "Where were we supposed to take that Egg again?"

The shadows of the forest were a great place to hide. A mysterious Pokémon with large, curved wings floated high in the branches, watching Ash and Pikachu. It stayed out of sight.

Just then, another Pokémon appeared. It was almost twice as tall as Ash and nearly three times as wide. And it was very, very pink. "Oh, wow," Ash said with a gasp.

"Pika!" Pikachu chirped in agreement.

The pink-and-grey Pokémon began to wave its large, log-like arms.

"Look, it's waving!" exclaimed Ash, approaching slowly. "You sure are cute."

The Pokémon appeared to be walking towards them with a friendly grin. Then suddenly it began to whirl around, breaking tree limbs with its gigantic paws. It let out an angry, high-pitched squeak.

"Move it!" Ash yelled, and he and Pikachu ran with all their might. They leaped over bushes and dodged trees until they came to a small clearing.

"What was that thing?" Ash wondered out loud. The super-sized Pokémon had seemed

so happy to see them at first.

Luckily, Ash didn't worry about it for long. It was only seconds before another Pokémon distracted him. He noticed a Charizard flying high above – with a person on its back!

"That must be an Air Ride Pokémon," Ash said. "That's awesome! Pikachu, let's follow it!"

Ash and Pikachu chased after the Fire- and Flying-type Pokémon. They soon emerged from the trees.

Ash stopped and took in the sight. Before him was a large field with a track around it. There were several grand buildings with thatched roofs and outdoor walkways. The grounds also included a lake and lots of tall palm trees. It was beautiful! And the best part? There were Pokémon everywhere.

Ash stepped forwards in awe. He didn't look before he crossed the track, and three racing Tauros came barrelling full steam ahead, nearly trampling him!

A girl with long blonde hair hurried towards him. "Are you OK?" she asked, worried. Pikachu rushed forward to check on him, too.

Ash laughed it off as he stood up. "Actually, I'm good at dealing with Tauros. See, I've caught some."

Soon, all the Tauros and their riders joined them, too. They all looked concerned.

"What is this place?" Ash asked.

"It's the Pokémon School," said a girl named Mallow.

"The Pokémon School," Ash repeated slowly. "Wow!"

CHAPTER 2

MEET THE CREW

"I've heard of the Pokémon School! I can't believe this is it," Ash said.

"I'll show you around," Mallow offered. She grabbed Ash by the hand and tugged. On her shoulder she had a small round Grass-type Pokémon called Bounsweet. It had a green stem on top of its head and gave off a deliciously sweet smell.

Mallow practically dragged Ash into one
of the big buildings. All around, there were
kids and Pokémon studying or playing
games. Ash could hardly believe it when
Mallow took him into a large room filled
with ancient Pokémon skeletons. There
were flying Pokémon skeletons hanging
from the ceiling; and there were other
Pokémon skeletons, built bone by bone, on

display on the wooden floor.

"This is great!" Ash exclaimed. "Where am I again?"

Mallow giggled. "I told you. It's the Pokémon School. It's a place where Pokémon and students all study together."

Next Mallow knocked on a closed door. "Principal, sir?" she called out. "I brought a new student."

Ash didn't have time to explain that he *wasn't* a new student before the door opened. Inside the office Ash saw a man and ... his mum!

"Ash! You finally made it," his mum said.

Ash realised that his mum had come to the school, too, on their errand for Professor Oak.

"Alola, Ash!" said the man, who looked very familiar. "Welcome to the Pokémon

School, home of SOLrock and roll!"

Ash was confused. "Professor Oak," he said. "What are you doing here?"

The man laughed out loud. "People tell me we look alike. The name is Samson Oak."

Ash realised that this man was Professor Oak's cousin – the person who was expecting the Egg that he and his mum had brought all the way from Pallet Town.

"He's the Pokémon School principal," Mallow explained.

"Nice to meet CHU!" Samson Oak said, making eye contact with Pikachu.

"He always makes jokes," Mallow said, slightly embarrassed. "He's always playing around with Pokémon names."

"We all need a little fun," Principal Oak said, smiling.

He set out to contact his cousin, Professor Oak. He wanted to tell him that the Egg had arrived safe and sound.

"Say, Principal Oak, sir," Mallow began. "May I show Ash around the campus?"

Ash held his breath, feeling hopeful.

"Of course! PoryGON your way ..."

Ash was already getting used to the principal's odd way of putting Pokémon names into everything he said. Porygon was a Virtual Pokémon from his home region of Kanto.

"Now, this is our classroom," Mallow said, as they entered a gigantic room with high ceilings and windows open to the tropical air.

"Hi!" said a young man. He was wearing a lab coat, board shorts and a cap. "A big Alola to you all!"

"Professor Kukui!" Mallow looked happy to see him.

"Professor?" Ash mumbled. He didn't know any professors who wore a lab coat – without a shirt.

"Yeah, he's our teacher! Professor, I'd like you to meet Ash," Mallow said.

"Principal Oak just filled me in," the teacher said. "Hi, Ash and Pikachu. I hope you enjoy your visit here!"

Ash was pretty sure he would. "Thank you!"

When Mallow, Ash and Pikachu went outside, they noticed the same Charizard that Ash had originally followed out of the forest, and the guy who had been riding it was there. "That's Kiawe," Mallow said. Kiawe and Charizard were students at the Pokémon School, too.

Soon they were joined by the same group of students that Ash had met when he first arrived on school grounds. Mallow introduced Lillie, the girl with the long blonde hair who had first approached him; Lana, who always carried Popplio, the Sea Lion Pokémon, in her arms; and Sophocles and the Roly-Poly Pokémon Togedemaru, who both looked very alike.

With Kiawe and Mallow, that was the

Pokémon School class! Professor Kukui had come down to meet his students.

Ash noticed a cool band around Kiawe's wrist. It contained a crystal.

Professor Kukui explained that the band was called a Z-Ring. It was made of square metal plates, with a crystal in the centre of the largest plate. Kiawe had earned the Z-Ring in a ceremony called the Island Challenge, and now he and his Charizard were able to do an epic, overpowering move called a Z-Move.

There was so much to learn about the Pokémon of the Alola region. Ash hoped he and Pikachu would have enough time on their holiday to learn it all.

CHAPTER 3

TAPU KOKO, SPIRIT GUARDIAN

Ash was chatting to the students outside the Pokémon School when he saw something flash by in the air. It was colorful, with bright patterns, and it was fast. The sight of it gave him a thrill. Then it disappeared behind a cluster of trees.

"Who's that Pokémon?" Ash asked.

"Pokémon?" Sophocles questioned, looking all around.

"I don't see anything," Mallow said.

But Ash knew he had seen it. It was odd, but he felt sure that the Pokémon had been watching them. "It was just there," he insisted. "It was a Pokémon for sure! It was yellow, about this big." Ash motioned with his arms. "It had a big orange crest on its head." He could still see it in his mind.

The rest of the group looked sceptical.

Professor Kukui frowned and then said, "That sounds like—"

"Tapu Koko," Kiawe finished.

"You saw Tapu Koko, Guardian of Melemele Island?" Lillie questioned.

"Wow. A guardian? That's what that was?" Ash replied. He sounded equally stunned.

Little did they know that Tapu Koko

had been watching Ash. Earlier that day, Tapu Koko had seen Ash in the forest. It was interested in Ash's fascination with Pokémon. But why would the Guardian of Melemele Island be so curious about Ash?

Later that night, Ash and his mum were having dinner on the hotel terrace.

"Anything interesting happen today?" Ash's mum asked, but Ash was lost in all his incredible memories from that afternoon. "You seem a little distracted this evening."

Just then, Ash heard a trilling coo. Pikachu heard it, too. Ash knew at once what it was. He rushed to the terrace railing.

He saw a flash of yellow and orange, and the striking triangular marking on its wings.

Ash didn't hesitate – he leapt over the railing and took off.

"Where are you going?" his mum called.

Pikachu bounded behind Ash as they tracked down the flying Pokémon. Ash spotted it high above, so he climbed a tall staircase that wound up around a lush hillside. At the top, Ash found an empty plaza. Tapu Koko hovered above the plaza.

Ash was in awe. Tapu Koko floated in the air without flapping its wide, curved wings.

The Pokémon looked at Ash. Its markings made it look like a warrior, bold and proud.

Ash felt a connection. "How come only I can see you? Is there something you want to tell me?"

The majestic Pokémon cooed again. Then it released something from its wing. It was a band with a brilliant crystal at the centre.

"Whoa, that looks like the Z-Ring Kiawe was wearing," Ash said. He looked up at the Spirit Guardian. Tapu Koko nodded.

When Ash reached out and grabbed the band, it sent a rush of electricity through him. A gleaming light circled the Z-Ring.

Ash could tell it was powerful, but he didn't fully understand why. He had many more questions, but the Spirit Guardian gracefully flew away, leaving Ash and Pikachu alone.

CHAPTER 4

ELECTRIUM Z

After that experience, it wasn't surprising that Ash wanted to stay in Alola to learn more about Tapu Koko and all the other new Pokémon there. As soon as Ash told his mum, she helped make the arrangements. She knew her son well, and she had a feeling he would love the chance to be a student at the Pokémon School.

One of the best parts was that Ash would be able to stay with Professor Kukui, and he'd be with Mallow, Kiawe, Lillie and the others in Professor Kukui's class. It was such an amazing opportunity. Both Ash and Pikachu were excited for all the adventures they'd experience in Alola.

Professor Kukui's classroom was in full swing before Ash and Pikachu arrived on their first day. Mallow and Lillie were working together to develop a new recipe for Pokémon food. Mallow's family ran a local restaurant, and she had grown up creating all kinds of tasty food, so she knew what ingredients would make a Pokémon meal super delicious. With Lillie's incredible knowledge of Pokémon, she knew just what foods and vitamins would make a healthier snack.

"If you added Mago Berry or Aguav Berry, the food would be better balanced," Lillie suggested.

"Lillie, you're the best!" Mallow exclaimed. "I'll try it now. Thank you!"

Just then, Mallow's companion, Bounsweet, jumped gleefully onto Mallow's shoulder. Lillie cried out in surprise.

"It's such a shame," Mallow said. "You know so much about Pokémon, but you can't touch them."

"I can touch them," Lillie insisted. "I theorize that it's only a matter of if I want to touch them or not."

Everyone found it strange that Lillie didn't like to touch Pokémon, because she was clearly fascinated by them. During lessons, Lillie always politely raised her hand and could answer almost any question

Professor Kukui or Principal Oak asked. She devoured Pokémon facts like a Snorlax with its favourite snack. But although she enjoyed learning about Pokémon in books or on the computer, if she encountered one in real life, she would yelp and jump back. She couldn't help it; it was a reflex.

That morning, Sophocles was working on a project with Togedemaru, his loyal Roly-Poly Pokémon. With his mechanical mind, Sophocles often tried to figure out how things work, and Togedemaru was a willing helper. Sophocles scratched his head and then hit one last key on his laptop.

"Togedemaru, charge program," Sophocles announced. "Execute!" He hit the final key, and Togedemaru jumped on a spinning wheel. Within seconds, the motion of the spinning wheel had created enough

energy to power up a lightbulb! Sophocles
liked classroom time, where he could be
in charge of experiments. He didn't have
nearly the same energy for fieldwork and
catching Pokémon in the wild.

"Popplio, make a balloon!" Lana directed.
She and Popplio, the Sea Lion Pokémon,
were just enjoying each other's company.
Lana was working with Popplio on blowing
giant bubbles from his round, bright-pink
nose. With each of Popplio's tries, she

would shield her face as soon as the bubble burst, and then giggle.

Kiawe was one of the last to arrive. He had already taken care of a delivery job that morning, all the way to Ula'ula Island!

"That's far away," Sophocles said.

"With my Charizard, it takes no time at all," Kiawe admitted, as he took his seat and faced the front of the classroom.

It was clear that all the students at the Pokémon School were devoted to Pokémon, and they all wanted to learn more about how people and Pokémon can work together. Ash and Pikachu would fit right in.

"Alola!" Ash called as soon as he entered the room.

"Alola," the other students responded.

"Starting today, Ash will be joining us at the Pokémon School," Professor Kukui explained. "If he has any questions, please don't hesitate to help him out."

"See, I really want to become a Pokémon Master! So I want to learn everything about this place," Ash told his classmates. He was certain that spending time with everyone at the Pokémon School would get him one step closer to his dream.

At once, a crowd gathered around Ash. "That's so cool," Sophocles said, motioning to the band on Ash's wrist. "Is that a Z-Crystal?"

"Yeah," Kiawe said, stepping a little closer to the group. "It's an Electrium Z. Where did you get that? You didn't participate in the Island Challenge, did you?"

Ash remembered the explanation of Kiawe's band, called a Z-Ring, the day before. He knew what Kiawe had had to accomplish to earn it. "Tapu Koko gave it to me," Ash said awkwardly.

"Tapu Koko?" Kiawe sounded uncertain.

"You saw it again?" Mallow questioned.

They were all fascinated, so Ash told them about how the band had just come floating down to him. "Right out of the sky."

"Pika pika," Pikachu murmured in agreement.

"How could Tapu Koko have gotten a Z-Ring?" Kiawe wondered.

"It felt like ..." Ash paused. "It felt like Tapu Koko was telling me that the ring was for me."

The other students all reacted with amazement. Only Kiawe looked truly uncertain.

"I've read about Tapu Koko," Lillie told them. "Tapu Koko is well known as the guardian who likes to help islanders, but it also likes to play tricks on people." She took a deep breath. "I also read that on rare occasions it will give mysterious gifts to people it likes."

"So that must mean Tapu Koko really likes Ash!" Mallow said.

Ash hoped that was the case, but he also considered the other things that Lillie had told them. They didn't really know why Tapu Koko had given him the Z-Ring.

"Kiawe, hold on," Sophocles said. "You got your Z-Ring from the Akala Island Kahuna, right?"

"Yeah," Kiawe agreed. "By successfully passing the grand trial."

"That's awesome!" Ash couldn't contain his excitement. "Does this mean I can use Z-Moves just like you?"

"Using Z-Moves should not be taken lightly," Kiawe said. "Only when a Pokémon's and its Trainer's hearts become one will the Z-Ring turn their feelings into power. But those feelings must be about something greater than themselves. Like ..."

"Like what?" Ash prompted.

"Helping the islands, helping Pokémon," Kiawe continued, "or helping others. Only those who care about all living things in our world are permitted to use Z-Moves." Kiawe sounded stern but noble, as if he were standing up for something he believed in.

"I'm not exactly sure what Tapu Koko saw in you, but as a Z-Ring owner, you need to realize your responsibility."

Ash looked at the older student. The Z-Ring around Ash's wrist was shiny and angular. With its elaborate crystal, it looked very modern. The necklace around Kiawe's bare neck was different. It was made of ancient beads and artefacts, all strung on a rope of brown leather.

"I don't understand much of that complicated stuff," Ash admitted. "But I know how special the Z-Moves are. You can count on me. And that's about all I can say."

Kiawe smiled. "That's good enough."

CHAPTER 5

ALOLAN EXEGGUTOR

Professor Kukui called the class to order. That day, Principal Oak was teaching. His lesson was about how there were many Pokémon who look different in the Alola region. He started by pointing out the differences between the typical Exeggutor and the Exeggutor from Alola.

"Wow," said Sophocles. "Their heights are totally different."

"But their faces look the same," observed Lana.

They were both right. The principal went on to explain that the warm and sunny weather on the islands created an ideal environment for many Pokémon. "The phenomenon of Pokémon developing their distinct appearance based on the region in which they live is called 'regional variant'," the principal continued. He went on to tell the class that Exeggutor is usually a Grass- and Psychic-type.

When he asked what type Exeggutor in the Alola region was, Lillie was quick to answer. "A Grass- and Dragon-type," she called out.

"A Dragon-type Exeggutor!" Ash exclaimed, rushing forwards to look at the

long-necked Exeggutor up close. Its neck looked like the trunk of a palm tree and its tail looked like a thick branch.

"Whoa, there's something about its tail you should know…" Lillie started to say.

But Ash was already reaching out to touch the Pokémon's long tail. Quick as a flash, Exeggutor curved the end of its tail around to face Ash, and that was interesting, because the tail had a face of its own!

The face was round and lime green, with puckered lips and a foul expression. In an instant, the tail whipped back and lashed out at Ash, flinging him into the air. Ash smashed into a bookcase ladder, smacking against each rung as he fell. *Bam, bam, bam, bam, bam!*

"Oh, brother," Kiawe muttered.

Finally, Ash caught one of the ladder rungs so he didn't crash onto the floor.

"The tail of the Exeggutor has a mind of its own," Lillie informed them. "You need to be careful in case it decides to attack you, which is what I was trying to say before."

Ash slid down to the floor. "Next time, get to the point a little sooner, OK?"

It was clear Ash had a lot to learn about regional Pokémon, and he'd probably have to work hard to catch up with his classmates. But a spanking by a Grass- and Dragon-type Exeggutor's tail was not going to stop him!

Luckily, Professor Kukui made up for the trying day with a delicious meal back at his house. "It's called an Alola plate, it's a popular dish in this region."

Pikachu was adjusting well to life in Alola. It had made fast friends with Professor Kukui's favourite Pokémon, Rockruff. Rockruff was a Puppy Pokémon and it had a long history of living in harmony with people. This Rockruff liked to snuggle up to Ash and Pikachu, rubbing the rocks on its neck against them.

The next morning, Professor Kukui had already left for school when Ash woke up. Ash realised that he was running late, and it was only his second day! As he raced along the road, Pikachu bounded close behind.

As soon as they had reached the school's grand archway, they saw something blocking the entrance. Ash ran right into an object that was almost clear and felt like rubber. Whatever it was, it was expanding and pushing Ash away!

Suddenly it popped, and Ash and Pikachu fell backwards to the ground. "What was that?" Ash exclaimed, curious.

One by one, Ash's classmates appeared, looking very proud of themselves. When Ash saw Popplio there, he realised that he had run into one of the Sea Lion Pokémon's giant bubbles! But why?

"Alola surprise!" Mallow, Lillie and Lana yelled together.

"Did we surprise you?" Kiawe asked, offering Ash a hand up.

"You can say that again," Ash admitted.

"First off," Mallow began, "we decided today would be the perfect day to have a surprise welcome party for you! And that's just the first surprise."

"And next," Sophocles added in a gruff voice, "Togedemaru and I wanna challenge you."

"Challenge?" Ash said hopefully. "A Pokémon battle, right?"

Ash was thrilled at the idea of a real Pokémon battle. He and Pikachu made such a good team, and it would be a great way of proving himself in front of his new classmates. "OK, Sophocles, I accept your challenge! Right, Pikachu?"

"Pika!" Pikachu offered an excited squeak.

Ash and Pikachu were ready to show their stuff!

CHAPTER 6

CHALLENGE TIME

Ash and Pikachu looked at each other. They were both in their battle stance, but then they noticed two giant tubs of balloons. Sophocles stepped in front of one of the tubs and crossed his arms. Togedemaru was perched on his head.

Ash and Pikachu realized that it was

not going to be an ordinary Pokémon battle, but a kind of carnival game. What a bummer!

"Whichever team pops all the balloons first wins the game!" Mallow announced.

"Ready," Kiawe directed. "Go!"

Ash and Pikachu went in with a good attitude, but they struggled to pop even one balloon. Meanwhile, Sophocles was using the sharp spines on Togedemaru's back to pierce one balloon after another. *Pop, pop, pop!*

When Lillie told them they could use Pokémon powers, Ash jumped at the opportunity. "Let's pop them all with Thunderbolt!" he said.

As Pikachu charged up, Sophocles looked at Togedemaru. "All right, this is our chance!"

Pikachu shot into the air and blasted off a strong Thunderbolt move, but the bolt didn't zoom towards the balloons. Instead, Togedemaru seemed to absorb all the charge. The Roly-Poly Pokémon spun around the balloon tub in a super-fast whirl, bursting one balloon after another.

"Hey, what's that all about?" Ash asked.

"Here's the deal," Sophocles explained. "Togedemaru's ability is Lightning Rod. It absorbs lightning bolts with its spines. Then it releases those lightning bolts as a move."

"Wow ..." Ash said, amazed. "Togedemaru rocks!"

As soon as Mallow declared Sophocles and Togedemaru the winners, Lana told Ash what his next surprise would be: a challenge against Lana and Popplio, the Sea Lion Pokémon. It was going to be a Pokémon Aquathlon, a competition where the contestants run and then swim.

On land, Pikachu took a considerable lead. As Pikachu dove into the ocean, Ash yelled, "That's great, we're winning! Head for the finish line!"

But although Pikachu was speedy, Popplio was made for swimming. It had long fins for pushing through the water, and its body was aerodynamic. It took very little time for

Popplio to overtake Pikachu.

Popplio leaped triumphantly out of the water.

"Popplio can swim at speeds of twenty-five miles per hour," Lillie stated. "Very impressive."

"I can't believe how fast Popplio can move," Ash admitted. When Pikachu paddled up to land at last, Ash greeted him with a warm, dry towel. "Great, Pikachu! You rocked it."

The next challenge was a Tauros race against Kiawe. This really was not like any other school Ash had attended!

While the race was close, Ash came up short. When he dismounted, he gave Tauros a big pat. "Thanks," Ash said. "You're awesome."

"Pika!" Pikachu ran towards Ash.

"Thanks for cheering me on, buddy," Ash said. But Pikachu was no longer looking at him – Ash turned around to see that Professor Kukui was approaching them with Rockruff.

"You're now looking at your fifth surprise," the professor said. "If Pikachu agrees … let's battle!"

Ash could hardly believe it. "Whoa, a battle against Professor Kukui!"

Pikachu bounded onto Ash's shoulder in excitement.

"Before that," Mallow added, "I'm going to prepare us all a little lunch!"

All Ash really wanted was a Pokémon battle, but all of a sudden … "Um, come to think of it," he admitted. "I'm starving!"

At Mallow's family's restaurant, they all got their fill. "Delish!" said Ash, looking at all the colourful platters of food.

"Mallow's restaurant is really good," agreed Sophocles. "I don't like eating anywhere else."

Even the Pokémon had a tasty and healthy meal. They all ate off the same large plate.

Just as Ash was going to take another big bite, a high trill carried over the wind to the restaurant porch.

"What was that?" Ash mumbled, even though he was pretty sure what the sound was. He stood up and walked over to the edge of the porch, gazing into the forest.

Suddenly, there was a gentle swishing sound, and Tapu Koko appeared right in front of Ash. His classmates all gasped in surprise.

"Melemele's Island Guardian!" Lillie whispered in awe. "Tapu Koko!"

"What a sight!" Mallow said.

"Beautiful," Lana agreed.

All the Pokémon murmured in excitement, too.

Here was Tapu Koko, hovering before them – face-to-face with Ash. The Spirit Guardian regarded him with an intense gaze.

"It's great to see you," Ash said. "I didn't get a chance to thank you for the ring. So, thank you!" Ash held up his arm to show the Spirit Guardian that he was wearing it.

Tapu Koko answered with an inquisitive chirp. With a speedy swoosh, Tapu Koko rushed forward and snatched Ash's cap from his head, holding it tight in its sharp beak. Then it darted all around the porch.

"It's so fast, I can't see it," Ash said.

Tapu Koko dashed around playfully and

dropped the cap on Pikachu's head. Then Tapu Koko grabbed the hat back and jetted off into the forest. Even though it glided with great speed, it was nearly silent.

The students and their Pokémon stared in amazement as it flew into the forest.

CHAPTER 7

PIKACHU VS TAPU KOKO

"Hey, wait!" In an instant, Ash started to chase after Tapu Koko.

"Pika!" Pikachu called out to Ash as it followed its Trainer. All Ash's classmates and Professor Kukui joined them.

Tapu Koko easily weaved through the forest, floating over crystal-clear streams and fallen trees. Ash and Pikachu hurried to keep up.

When Ash arrived in a clearing, it seemed as if Tapu Koko had disappeared. Ash looked to the top of the trees, searching behind the jade-coloured leaves. "Huh?" he questioned. "Where is it? Where'd it go?"

Then, Tapu Koko appeared again ... and plopped the cap on Ash's head. It had one wing stretched out, as if it were pointing right at Ash and Pikachu.

"Hey, what's going on?" Ash wondered. "Do you want to have a battle with me?"

By this time, the group had gathered behind him, but Tapu Koko only seemed interested in Ash and Pikachu.

"A battle?" Kiawe sounded uncertain.

"So his fifth surprise isn't me," murmured Professor Kukui. "Guess it's Tapu Koko."

"I read about this sort of thing once," Lillie said. "Tapu Koko is a very curious Pokémon. Long ago, it would challenge islanders to Pokémon battles."

"All right, you've got yourself a deal," Ash said, looking right at the Spirit Guardian. "Let's have a battle now!"

"Pika pika!" Pikachu chimed in.

At once, Tapu Koko spread its wings wide, and a mystical force radiated across the forest floor. It put an electric yellow haze on everything.

Professor Kukui gasped. "That's Electric Terrain," he said.

"Ash!" Lillie yelled, quickly. "Electric-type moves become more powerful while Electric Terrain is in effect!"

"Lucky for us," Ash replied. "All right!"

But before Ash could call a move,

Tapu Koko dove forward, aiming right for Pikachu! The Spirit Guardian glowed with a bright, multicoloured force. It hit Pikachu head-on, and the little Electric-type Pokémon tumbled backwards.

Tapu Koko spun around and took aim again.

"Down, Pikachu!" Ash cried. Pikachu ducked for cover. "Now, let's show them what we can do," Ash directed. "Pikachu, use Thunderbolt!"

"Pi-ka-chuuuu!" the Mouse Pokémon cried as it charged up.

Pikachu's charge surrounded the Spirit Guardian, but when the power fizzled away, Tapu Koko still floated there, unchanged.

"It didn't do a thing," Ash mumbled in disbelief.

"Tapu Koko's just too strong," Kiawe said.

When the Spirit Guardian rushed towards
Ash, the young Trainer shielded himself.
But the powerful Pokémon just stopped in
front of him and gently brushed its wing
against the Z-Ring. At its touch, the ring
began to glow.

"You want me to use it?" Ash asked.

Tapu Koko made a light whirring coo,
encouraging Ash.

"The Z-Ring and Electrium Z?" he said

softly. "I have no idea how to do it, but I'll try. OK Pikachu. Let's show our Z-Move!" Ash took his stance, and Pikachu got ready.

"Oh, Ash," Mallow murmured with concern.

"Can they do it? I wonder," Sophocles said.

"All right." Ash crossed his arms, and the Z-Ring seemed to glow brighter. Pikachu stood up, balling its paws into fists. Pikachu and Ash seemed to move with the same powerful strides as they geared up for their Z-Move.

At last, Ash called, "Go, Pikachu!"

"Pika pikaaaa!" The Mouse Pokémon was determined, its zigzagged tail flicking with energy. Just as Ash thrust his clenched fist forwards, Pikachu did the same.

"Here we go," Ash grunted. "Full ... power ... NOW!"

A ball of brilliant electricity zapped from Pikachu's paw and zoomed toward Tapu Koko.

"The Electric-type Z-Move!" Kiawe gasped.

"That was Gigavolt Havoc," Professor Kukui confirmed. "Wow!"

On the other side of the clearing, Pikachu's Electro Ball seemed to explode with a bright bang. The explosion sent a gush of wind in all directions. Pikachu was limp with exhaustion. The Z-Move took a lot of power.

"That was a Z-Move?" Ash said. "Oh, man."

When the dust had cleared, Ash and Pikachu could see a crater in the ground. The Z-Move had left a trail of broken soil, and the explosion had blown a deep hole in the forest floor.

Despite the destruction, Tapu Koko

hovered in the clearing, unharmed. The Spirit Guardian gave them a reassuring coo. And then, in an instant, it was gone.

The next thing Ash knew, his classmates and Professor Kukui were all rushing towards him.

"Are you OK?" Mallow asked.

"Yeah," Ash answered.

"I can't believe how strong you and Pikachu are," Mallow added, saying what all the students were thinking.

Kiawe noticed something. "What happened to your Z-Crystal?" he asked. "It's disintegrated."

Ash took a close look at his Z-Ring and saw that Kiawe was right.

"That means it's too soon for you to use Z-Moves," Kiawe said plainly. "You haven't had an Island Challenge yet."

Ash took a deep breath. He didn't fully understand the power of the Z-Move, but he knew that he and Pikachu could master it, eventually.

"All right," Ash said gamely. "I'll take the Island Challenge trial!"

The others seemed surprised at Ash's willing attitude.

"I'll pass the trial, and I'll get another Z-Crystal, and then I'll be able to use Z-Moves ... the right way!"

"Sounds perfect," Mallow declared. "We'll all be cheering for you." Bounsweet gave a chirp of approval. The rest of the students – except for Kiawe – all agreed.

"Togedemaru and I know lots about Electric-types," Sophocles offered. "TONS of stuff."

There was one student whose help Ash

needed the most. He needed a mentor, someone who knew all about how Z-Moves work. He turned to Kiawe. "Please?" he said.

Kiawe still looked reluctant. "Well, I guess I have to," he replied. "After all, I'm the only one of us with a Z-Ring."

"Yay!" cheered Lana.

Pikachu chirped in gratitude. "Pika pika!"

"That's awesome!" Ash said. "Thanks, guys."

Now Ash and Pikachu had a new goal for their time in Alola. And they had a team of helpful friends to help them along the way.

CHAPTER 8

ENTER ROTOM DEX

"Ash, I have something for you," Professor Kukui said later that day. They were both relaxing in his home. The teacher held out his hand. "A present," Professor Kukui said, holding out a red gadget.

"What is it?" Ash asked.

"It's a Pokédex," the professor answered.

"Wow!" Ash replied. It wasn't like any Pokédex he had seen before. Regardless, it was the perfect gift. With all the new Pokémon Ash hoped to encounter in Alola, a Pokédex would be super handy.

Next, Professor Kukui said it was time to activate the Pokédex, and he led Ash downstairs to his office.

"Perfect!" the professor announced, as he tapped a return button on his computer keyboard. A series of codes flashed across the computer screen. "We're all connected!"

Lights began to flicker and an odd electric current seemed to jump between the computer and the other machines. "Here it comes!" announced Professor Kukui.

The lights blacked out and then surged back on. The crackle of static filled the air. "What's going on?" Ash asked.

"Just hang on and you'll see,"
Professor Kukui responded confidently.

Ash saw it out of the corner of his eye.
Something slipped from the electric socket.
It swooshed around at top speed, beeping
all the way. "It's a Rotom!" Ash exlaimed.
Rotom had the power to live inside various
electronic devices.

"Now we just have to wait for Rotom to go
inside," said Professor Kukui.

"Go inside?" Ash repeated. "Inside the Pokédex?" Now this was getting interesting. With a zip and a zing, Rotom bounced around the office, finally whizzing straight into the Pokédex.

"Whoa! Is Rotom in there?" Ash asked, knocking on the red gadget. Eyes appeared on the device, and then the eyes opened! Arms and legs sprouted, and the Pokédex's face blinked to life.

"The Pokédex is Rotom and Rotom is the Pokédex!" Ash said in amazement.

The Pokédex seemed to be beeping a friendly hello.

"Alola, Rotom!" Ash said with a wave.

"Pika, pika!" Pikachu greeted the device.

"Language selection complete," the Pokédex stated.

"Wow," Ash said. "Rotom just talked!"

Professor Kukui stepped forwards and helped with the introductions. "Rotom, please lend Ash a helping hand from now on, OK?"

"Understood," replied Rotom. "Ash, user registration complete. Pokédex now booting up." The device made a whirring noise, then it clicked. "Now at 100 percent. Nice to meet you, Ash!"

"Wow, we can even have a conversation?" Ash said in awe.

"Of course. Rotom Dex has been programmed to communicate properly with people of all different kinds."

"Awesome," Ash said.

"Awesome?" Rotom Dex repeated. An odd look crossed its face. It appeared to be confused. "Awesome does not compute."

"Ash was just saying that he is very

impressed with your capabilities," Professor Kukui explained.

"I understand," confirmed Rotom Dex. "So awesome means excellent. And that means Rotom Dex is excellent!"

Professor Kukui and Ash introduced it to Pikachu and Rockruff. Rotom Dex took pictures of both Pokémon to record them into its memory. It explained that it was a "self-learning" Pokédex that updated its data every time it met a new Pokémon.

Ash asked Rotom Dex to describe Pikachu using the information it had in its Pokédex.

"Right away, Ash," responded Rotom Dex. "Pikachu. The Mouse Pokémon. An Electric-type. It raises its tail to sense its surroundings. If you pull its tail, it will bite."

"Pika!" Pikachu, who was sitting on Ash's shoulder, was impressed. Rotom Dex hovered over to Pikachu and pulled its tail. Surprised, Pikachu sent out an electric pulse. It shocked both Rotom Dex and Ash! They both yelped. Yikes!

"It doesn't bite you," Rotom Dex corrected, still shaking. "It actually shocks you."

Ash could tell that Rotom Dex would be an amazing help during his adventures in Alola.

Meanwhile, some of Ash's old enemies had just arrived on Melemele Island. Fresh off the plane, Team Rocket might have been in a new place, but they were still up to no good. And as always, they liked to announce their evil plans for the whole world to hear.

"This great and distant land gives us a brand-new start," James declared.

"Yeah, we're gonna do everything for the greatest Boss in Bossland," added Meowth with a greedy grin. Their "Boss" was the treacherous Giovanni, the notorious Gym Leader who wanted to collect all the rare Pokémon at any cost. Giovanni sent his minions Jessie, James, Meowth and Wobbuffet on missions to gather any and all powerful Pokémon.

Their mission in Alola was the same as always. Giovanni had demanded, "Go and collect Pokémon the likes of which I've never seen before!"

Team Rocket didn't even stop for a stroll on the beach or a fruity drink by the pool. They quickly got to work tracking down Alola's most exotic Pokémon!

CHAPTER 9

TEAM ROCKET TROUBLE

Not far away at the Pokémon School, Ash and Professor Kukui were sharing Rotom Dex with the rest of the class. The students were amazed at the unique device.

"A Pokédex that operates with a Rotom inside," Lillie said to herself. "That's incredible!"

"Incredible," Rotom Dex repeated.
"Incredible means ... awesome. In other
words, Rotom Dex is awesome!"

"So it's obviously learned how Ash talks.
I wonder just how this Rotom Dex is
programmed." Sophocles approached
Rotom Dex with a screwdriver and a
mischievous grin. "I'm going to analyze your
programming for just a second, all right?"

"No, thank you," replied Rotom Dex.

"Ah, come on," Sophocles begged. "Just a
look?"

"No, I refuse!" Rotom Dex insisted.

Professor Kukui announced that they
would use this new device to help them with
the day's fieldwork lesson. Their aim: to
catch wild Pokémon!

"I just adore fieldwork," Mallow said.

The whole class set out with the awesome

Rotom Dex right at Ash's side. Ash hoped he would get to catch a wild Pokémon that would want to be part of his team.

But little did the students know they would soon meet up with unwanted company – the class was headed to the same part of the forest as Team Rocket.

As always, Jessie and James had big ambitions, but few practical plans.

"We'll snatch every Pokémon in the order we encounter them," declared James.

"Yeah," replied Meowth. "But that means that Wobbuffet and I are gonna have to do all the heavy lifting."

"There's no other choice," Jessie said. "We've left all the other Pokémon way back at Team Rocket headquarters. Even so ..." she added, looking around nervously. "It's kind of creepy out here. It feels like something scary could jump out at any moment."

Then suddenly something did! There was a strange Pokémon on the path up ahead.

"Pikachu?" Jessie asked, uncertain.

"Yipes!" said Meowth. The Pokémon looked like Pikachu, but not exactly. Its head was wobbly, and the eyes and mouth on its face looked odd, like they were drawn on. The Pokémon made a scritchy-scratchy sound that sent chills down Meowth's spine. "Giving it a closer look, it's a different Pokémon wearing a Pikachu-like thingy."

"Woooooobbuffet." Even Wobbuffet was frightened of the unknown Pokémon.

"What's wrong with you two?" Jessie demanded. "Meowth, what is it saying?"

Meowth refused to answer. "Something so scary that it's better not to know."

"Scary? It's not that scary," Jessie insisted. "It's kind of cute. So our very first job in the Alola region will be catching that cutie!" She grabbed Meowth and flung him across the forest. "Meowth. Fury Swipes! Let's go!"

As Meowth flew through the air, he launched his Fury Swipes move. With his claws out he yelled, "Desperate measures!"

He was sure he got some good swipes in, but the other Pokémon was unaffected.

"Ch-choo, ch-choo," the other Pokémon growled.

"Will you knock off all of the scary talk?" Meowth demanded. "Take off that Pikachu getup and fight fair and square!" He tackled the unknown Pokémon, pulling up its disguise slightly.

At that moment, something mysterious happened. Meowth passed out, as if he'd breathed a powerful gas. Whatever it was, it appeared to have come from under the other Pokémon's disguise. Meowth was unconscious!

Finally, James and Jessie manged to shake Meowth awake. Then they heard someone approaching. Jessie, James, Meowth and Wobbuffet scrambled into the bushes to spy on whoever was coming their way.

CHAPTER 10

PIKACHU VS MEOWTH

"I've got the feeling we'll run into some Pokémon soon," Ash said, as the students of the Pokémon School walked along one of the forest trails.

"The probability of meeting a Pokémon in this area is 83.9 percent," Rotom Dex announced.

"Over there!" Ash called out, pointing down the path towards the Pokémon in a Pikachu costume.

"Looks like your feeling was right," Mallow said.

"It's a Mimikyu," Lillie announced.

"Mimikyu," Rotom Dex took over. "The Disguise Pokémon. A Ghost- and Fairy-type. It wears a ragged head cover to look like a Pikachu, but little is known about this Pokémon. It is said that a scholar who once tried to look under the disguise met his end."

Even though Mimikyu sounded dangerous, Ash still wanted to try to catch it. "All right, Pikachu, go and get Mimikyu!"

"Pikachu, use Iron Tail," Ash directed, and Pikachu bounded forwards, its tail glowing a shiny silver.

Mimikyu lashed back with an attack of its own, rushing towards Pikachu in a full-on tackle. Before Pikachu had fully recovered, Mimikyu targeted a second attack right at Pikachu. The Mouse Pokémon landed flat on its back.

In the bushes, Jessie and James couldn't contain their excitement. "Did you just see that? That Mimikyu, or whatever they called it, is strong," Jessie said.

"It appears quite the even match for the twerp's Pikachu," James agreed. At once, he and Jessie knew they couldn't let Ash catch such a strong Pokémon.

Just as Pikachu was going to launch another move, Team Rocket climbed out of the shrubs. "Just a minute!" Jessie interrupted.

"Who are you?" Kiawe asked.

Team Rocket started a long explanation of their villainous mission, but it was so wordy and extreme that none of the students or their Pokémon could follow it.

"Team Rocket? I've never heard of them," Mallow said, puzzled.

James huffed. "Team Rocket is a super-powerful evil organization," he explained.

Still, none of the students from Alola knew anything about them.

So Ash cleared it up. "They're bad guys who like to steal other people's Pokémon," he said simply. "You've come to the Alola region to do bad things here, too, right?"

Jessie rolled her eyes. "Same old, genius."

"And first we're going to take your Pikachu and all of your friends' Pokémon, too!" James threatened.

"And that Mimikyu!" Jessie screeched. "We found that one before you."

"Watch out, Pikachu," Meowth yelled. "I know how strong you are, but today I come out on top! Fury Swipes!"

Ash quickly made a move. "Pikachu, Electro Ball!"

Pikachu's strike caught Meowth off-guard in midair. But then something unexpected happened. Mimikyu shuffled forwards and shot off a dark, powerful Shadow Ball that countered Pikachu's move.

"Call me crazy, but I get the strange feeling that Mimikyu is trying to help us out," Jessie said.

"Mimikyu, you came through like a champ," Meowth cheered. "Thanks, pal."

"Ch-ch-ch-ch-choo." Mimikyu appeared to agree.

"It's all good, Mimikyu, just attack!" Jessie screamed.

The whole Pokémon School braced for the attack on Pikachu.

"Now be careful," Rotom Dex called out.

"Here it comes," warned Ash.

Mimikyu was charging up a giant, super-powerful Shadow Ball. Jessie and James began to dance and cheer. But before Mimikyu was able to launch its move, a giant Pokémon grabbed Jessie and James from behind and began to carry them away.

"Hey, big guy, where are you taking my two buddies?" Meowth demanded.

"Who's that Pokémon?" Ash asked.

"Bewear," answered Rotom Dex. "The Strong Arm Pokémon. A Normal- and Fighting-type. Bewear has extremely powerful arms and it's very dangerous. It waves its arms in a friendly fashion, but this is a means of warning."

Ash remembered meeting the pink-and-grey Pokémon in the woods earlier. "Really dangerous," Ash agreed.

"Mimikyu, Wobbuffet, save Jessie and James! Move!" Meowth demanded.

With Meowth, Wobbuffet and Mimikyu hot on the trail of the Bewear, the Pokémon School crew could finally catch its breath.

While Ash and Kiawe regretted not being

able to catch Mimikyu, the others chose to look on the bright side.

"There are many, many other Pokémon in the Alola region," Lillie reminded them.

"The probability of finding a Pokémon in this part of the forest has increased to 96.5 percent," said Rotom Dex. With that news, Ash and Pikachu continued their quest.

CHAPTER 11

ENTER ROWLET

In Professor Kukui's class, the students were enjoying another chance to do fieldwork. It was a beautiful, sunny day, but Ash and his friends were deep in the shade of the forest once again. They hadn't seen any signs of Team Rocket since Bewear had carried off Jessie and James.

That was fine with Ash. He wanted to focus on his quest. Ash still hadn't managed to catch a wild Pokémon in Alola, but he was giving it his best shot.

"Grubbin, the Larva Pokémon. A Bug-type." Rotom Dex was giving Ash all the data on the Pokémon he was preparing to battle. "Grubbin scrapes trees with its jaws and drinks their sap. It makes its home underground."

"Thanks, Rotom Dex," Ash called out.

When Grubbin tried String Shot, Pikachu jumped up to avoid it. Then Ash directed Pikachu to try Thunderbolt. The move was too much for Grubbin, and it collapsed on the ground.

Ash quickly grabbed a Poké Ball and tossed it.

Ash's classmates were cheering him on.

They all watched closely to see if Ash had made his first catch in Alola. But at the last moment, the Grubbin escaped the Poké Ball and dove into the ground.

They could follow where Grubbin was burrowing by its trail of upturned dirt. "Quick, Pikachu!" Ash called. "Aim where Grubbin is about to come out."

But the Larva Pokémon had come out of the ground all the way across the clearing. It launched a String Shot move and captured Pikachu by the leg, speedily reeling in Ash's Pokémon.

"Watch out for its powerful jaws!" Rotom Dex warned, but it was too late. The Larva Pokémon snapped its pincer-like jaws, then dug another escape route.

Ash rushed over. "Are you OK?" he asked, leaning over Pikachu.

It was clear that Pikachu was dazed. Everyone agreed that Ash and Pikachu should go to the Pokémon Center for a check-up.

Pikachu was as good as new after the visit to the Pokémon Center. By the next day, Ash was already thinking about his Pokémon quest. "Today's the day!" he said to Mallow. They were sitting on the porch of her family's restaurant. "I'm catching a Pokémon for sure."

"The current Pokémon encounter rate in the forest is 89 percent," said Rotom Dex.

"That just might work," Mallow said, taking a piece of fruit. "The forest is where I first came across Bounsweet."

At that moment, a shadow seemed to block out the sun. "What is that?" Ash wondered, looking up. He saw a big flock of tiny flying Pokémon, and they were headed their way!

"Oh!" exclaimed Mallow. "It must be time for the Pikipek flocks! Around this time, Pikipek gather and store their food for the coming year. They travel in large flocks and harvest food wherever they can find it." She looked up at the sky. "I think they're coming for our fruit. It's a good thing we have lots of it."

Mallow and Ash watched as the little

Pokémon swooped in and grabbed the fruit with their feet. When the flock had gone, there wasn't a piece of fruit left.

But there was still one Normal- and Flying-type Pokémon looking for fruit. It flew down to the porch and aimed right for Bounsweet!

Luckily, Bounsweet was prepared with a cool spinning move that knocked it away.

"Hey! Who's that Pokémon?" Ash asked.

"Rowlet," answered Rotom Dex. "Rowlet is the Grass Quill Pokémon, a Grass- and Flying-type. It swoops down without making a sound and unleashes a powerful kick."

Rowlet aimed again for Bounsweet. And again, Bounsweet used its spinning move to defend itself.

Mallow explained that Bounsweet was always on guard. Because Bounsweet smelled like a delicious fruit, it needed good defenses.

"Lured by its scent, many flying Pokémon mistake Bounsweet for a berry," Rotom Dex confirmed. "Rowlet is attacking again!"

This time, Bounsweet's Spin knocked the Rowlet all the way to the electrical wire, where it grabbed ahold.

"Maybe that Rowlet's hungry," Ash thought out loud. When he looked up, he saw that Rowlet had lost hold of the wire and was falling. Ash dashed off the porch and made a leaping catch just before it hit the ground.

Mallow brought more fruit from inside.

"Are you OK?" Ash asked.

Rowlet responded with a quiet trill. The next moment, Rowlet discovered a bowl of melon and devoured it all.

"Want this, too?" Ash asked, offering a

banana. Rowlet grasped onto Ash's arm and gulped down the banana. "Man, you've got a strong grip." Ash reached out to give its feathers a pat. "You're so soft," he said, feeling his heart warm to the Grass Quill Pokémon. He took a Poké Ball in one hand. "Rowlet, is it OK if I catch—"

Before Ash could finish his sentence, Rowlet grabbed a watermelon and took off into the sky.

"Are you going to catch it?" Rotom Dex asked.

"You bet!" Ash replied. "Let's go!"

Not far away in the forest, Team Rocket was trapped in Bewear's den. The Strong Arm Pokémon was keeping them captive. It was looking after them and feeding them well, but it wouldn't let them go.

The good news though, for Team Rocket at least, was that Jessie had captured Mimikyu in one of James's Luxury Balls. And, for once, it appeared as if Bewear wasn't guarding the den door ...

"This is our chance," James said.

But just as Team Rocket was sneaking out, a flock of Pikipek swarmed into the den. The Pikipek quickly located Bewear's fruit stash, collected it and flew away.

Team Rocket was shocked.

"They took Bewear's food!" Meowth said.

"Let's get it back!" Jessie said. "Bewear might have captured us, but we owe it for feeding us and giving us shelter."

So Team Rocket hurried after the Pikipek.

CHAPTER 12

FOREST BATTLE

"There it is!" Ash called out. "Over there!"
Ash, Pikachu, Mallow, Bounsweet and
Rotom Dex had all chased Rowlet deep into
the forest. When they finally caught up with
the Grass Quill Pokémon, they saw that it
was in a nest with the flock of Pikipek, plus
a Trumbeak and a Toucannon.

"Here's where I come in." Rotom Dex began giving data on Pikipek, the Woodpecker Pokémon. "It can unleash sixteen pecks per second to drill a hole into a tree where it stores its food."

Next came information on Trumbeak, the Bugle Beak Pokémon. Trumbeak was the evolved form of Pikipek and could attack with seeds stored in its beak. Finally, Rotom Dex shared data on Toucannon, the evolved form of Trumbeak. "Toucannon's beak heats up to over two hundred degrees," Rotom Dex stated, "and its peck can inflict a serious burn."

Ash was watching Rowlet interact with the other Pokémon. He now understood why Rowlet had taken the watermelon. He guessed that Rowlet had been with the other Pokémon since hatching, so it gathered fruit like the Pikipek.

When Rowlet noticed Ash, it flew over to him and nestled itself inside his backpack.

"Wow," Ash said to the Pokémon, "I had no idea you had so many awesome friends."

All at once, there were sounds of an attack. Giant nets fell on the Pikipek nests, trapping them.

"What's going on?" Ash questioned.

Team Rocket had arrived, and they had a

new plan. "Team Rocket, let's fight!" they said in chorus.

"Team Rocket, let Pikipek and the others go!" Ash demanded.

"Sorry," screeched Jessie, "but the twerp loses again. They stole Bewear's food and that's a no-no."

"So we're here to take it back," said James.

"And your Pikachu will make the perfect present for the Boss," Jessie warned. "Take it away, Mimikyu!"

She flung a Luxury Ball, and Mimikyu sprung out with its scritchy-scratchy sound. "Take care of them the way you know how!" Jessie cried.

Mimikyu charged up a Shadow Ball and whizzed it Pikachu's way.

"Pikachu, Electro Ball!" Ash called out. Then, over his shoulder, he whispered to Rowlet. "Now's the time to save your friends."

Rowlet took off for the Pikipek nests.

The Shadow Ball and Electro Ball cancelled out each other in midair. Ash called on Pikachu to do Iron Tail. Pikachu slashed at Mimikyu, but the other Pokémon didn't lose energy. Iron Tail had no effect on Mimikyu at all!

Meanwhile, Rowlet had been able to approach the nests without being detected. With a quick slice, the nets fell open and the Pikipek flew away to safety. Team Rocket saw them escaping, but they were not about to give up.

"Mimikyu!" screeched Jessie. "Quick, attack one more time!"

Mimikyu rushed forwards, catching Pikachu off-guard.

"Check out Mimikyu's Play Rough," Meowth bragged. Mimikyu attacked again, sending Pikachu flailing through the air to land with a thud.

Seizing the opportunity, Jessie shouted, "Mimikyu, wrap it up!"

Mimikyu attacked.

"Shadow Claw," Meowth said. "Cool!"

"It knows Shadow Claw, too!" James said.

"You OK, Pikachu?" Ash asked, worried. Pikachu was weak and couldn't get up.

Suddenly, Rowlet appeared overhead. A whirlwind of green leaves spun around it. Protected by the rush of wind, it dove down and lifted Pikachu from the forest floor.

When Mimikyu's Shadow Claw hit, Pikachu was no longer there.

"Nice job!" Ash said. "Pikachu, you OK?"

"Pika!" the little Pokémon replied.

"Then, let's go!" Ash called. "Thunderbolt!" The strike hit Mimikyu. The mysterious Pokémon was rattled, but not exhausted.

As Rowlet rushed over to release Trumbeak and Toucannon, Mimikyu warmed up a Shadow Ball.

But at that very moment, Bewear appeared. Bewear plucked Wobbuffet, Meowth, James and Jesse clear off the ground. Then it picked up Mimikyu, too.

"Is this—" Jessie began with disbelief.

"—déjà vu?" James finished.

"Bewear, bewear," Bewear murmured innocently as it carried Team Rocket away.

Jessie and James groaned.

Pikipek surrounded Rowlet in a celebratory circle. Even Trumbeak was there, hugging the Grass Quill Pokémon.

"Rowlet looks so happy," Ash observed.

"It's wonderful," Mallow agreed.

Ash called to Rowlet. It flew up to him at once. Ash had Pikachu on one shoulder and Rowlet on the other. It felt nice.

"Thanks, Rowlet," Ash said. "Everybody's fine, thanks to you." He knelt down and helped Rowlet back to the ground, next to its friends. It wasn't easy. Ash had grown fond of the young Pokémon.

"OK, guys," he said to Mallow and the others. "Let's go home."

"Going home?" questioned Rotom Dex. "I thought you were going to catch Rowlet."

"It's OK," Ash insisted. "The thing is, Rowlet has a lot of friends. Look at them. They're a family."

Mallow seemed uncertain.

Toucannon did, too. It reached out and nudged Rowlet with its beak.

Rowlet cooed and took off, flying right up to land in Ash's backpack.

"Rowlet, what's up?" Ash asked, looking over his shoulder.

Rowlet lifted its wing, motioning to all its friends who were waving farewell.

Ash paused. "Rowlet, are you saying that you want to come with me?" he asked.

Rowlet trilled and rubbed its soft head against Ash's cheek.

"Awesome!" Ash exclaimed. He pulled a Poké Ball from his pocket. "You really want me to catch you?" he asked.

Rowlet trilled.

"All right. Here we go, Rowlet. Go Poké Ball!" Ash flung it into the air.

"I just caught a Rowlet!" Ash cheered. But as quickly as he had caught Rowlet, he let the Pokémon out of its Poké Ball.

Rowlet snuggled into Ash's backpack, and Pikachu sat on his shoulder. Ash couldn't imagine anything better.

Ash had caught his first Pokémon in Alola, but his adventures in the beautiful tropical region had just begun. Ash had many plans and had set many goals for himself while he was there. With Rowlet and Pikachu on his team – and the help of Rotom Dex and all his Pokémon School friends – Ash knew he had an amazing journey ahead of him!

FIND OUT HOW ASH'S ALOLAN
ADVENTURE CONTINUES IN

ALOLAN CHALLENGE

READ ON FOR A SNEAK PEAK ...

For ten-year-old Ash Ketchum, every day was
a step on his grand journey to becoming
a Pokémon Master. Since he'd arrived in
the Alola region, Ash had enrolled in the
Pokémon School, where he and Pikachu
had met many new friends and Pokémon.
Each and every day, they were learning new
things and having exciting adventures.

Ash and Pikachu loved exploring Alola.
One of Ash's favourite parts of being in
a new place was discovering all the new
Pokémon. Since they'd first come to Alola,

they'd met many new Pokémon friends and they'd also found a new battling partner for their team. The adorable Rowlet was a Grass- and Flying-type Pokémon with a knack for sneaking up on opponents ... and then sleeping away the rest of the day in Ash's backpack!

One morning, Ash was on his way to school when he encountered a Pokémon he hadn't seen before. It stared at him with its intense yellow eyes. Ash stared right back.

In no time, Rotom Dex gave Ash the lowdown on the Pokémon. "Litten. The Fire Cat Pokémon," Rotom Dex announced, hovering in the air just behind Ash. "A Fire-type. Litten show few emotions and prefer being alone."

Rotom Dex was a unique companion for Ash. Rotom was a Pokémon that had the ability to live inside various electronic devices. This Rotom was a present from Ash's teacher, Professor Kukui. Rotom had slipped straight from a plug socket and into a Pokédex. Now it was an amazing talking device that kept Ash informed about all the unknown Pokémon in Alola. Ash took Rotom Dex with him almost everywhere.

Litten stood on top of a stone wall and kept its steely eyes on Ash. Ash knelt down, trying to lure it his way.

"Litten takes time to build any level of trust," Rotom Dex told Ash.

Ash heard Rotom, but he still wanted to try to make friends with the cute Litten.

Litten jumped down from the wall and approached Ash.

"Hi. What's up?" Ash said, holding out his hand.

Without hesitating, Litten began to rub up against Ash's knees. Pikachu watched from its perch on Ash's shoulder.

"Hey, maybe you're hungry!" Ash said. He opened his backpack and pulled something out. "See? It's my lunch," he explained to the curious Litten.

READ ALOLAN CHALLENGE TO FIND
OUT WHAT HAPPENS NEXT!

WHICH POKÉMON DID YOU FIND IN THIS ADVENTURE?

☐ MIMIKYU

☐ ROWLET

☐ BEWEAR

Find information on lots of Pokémon
in the Official Pokémon Encyclopedia!

LOOK OUT FOR THESE OTHER OFFICIAL POKÉMON BOOKS